To Ben, Emily, and Simeon   M.J.

For Timothy, with love   A.C.

OXFORD
UNIVERSITY PRESS

Great Clarendon Street, Oxford OX2 6DP

Oxford University Press is a department of the University of Oxford.
It furthers the University's objective of excellence in research, scholarship,
and education by publishing worldwide in

Oxford New York

Auckland Bangkok Buenos Aires Cape Town Chennai
Dar es Salaam Delhi Hong Kong Istanbul Karachi Kolkata
Kuala Lumpur Madrid Melbourne Mexico City Mumbai Nairobi
São Paulo Shanghai Taipei Tokyo Toronto

Oxford is a registered trade mark of Oxford University Press
in the UK and in certain other countries

Text © Maurice Jones 2003
Illustrations © Anna Currey 2003

The author and illustrator have asserted their moral right to be
known as author and illustrator of the work.
Database right Oxford University Press (maker)
First published in 2003

British Library Cataloguing in Publication Data available

ISBN 0–19–279058-7 Hardback
ISBN 0–19–272421-5 Paperback

3 5 7 9 10 8 6 4 2

Typeset in Caslon 540
Printed in Malaysia

Little Bear
Finds a Friend

Maurice Jones

Illustrated by Anna Currey

OXFORD
UNIVERSITY PRESS

Little Bear wanted to explore.

He had seen the trees, and
the grass and the river.

He stared up at the snow-topped mountain.
'Maybe I'll find a new friend there,'
he thought.

So he set off to have a look.

The sun was warm, and Little Bear grew tired
so he sat down on a hollow log.

The log
was teeming
with shiny ants.

'Where are you going?' asked the ants.
'To the top of the mountain to explore,'
said Little Bear. 'Do you want to
come with me?'
'Sorry – too busy,'
the ants said.

So Little Bear went on his way.

But one little ant had nothing to do,
so he followed Little Bear.

Little Bear came to the edge of a huge forest.
The treetops were full of monkeys,
leaping from branch to branch.

'Where are you going?'
called the monkeys.

'To the top of the
mountain to explore,'
said Little Bear. 'Do you
want to come with me?'

'Not now,' chattered the
monkeys, 'we're having
too much fun!'

So Little Bear went on his way.

But one little monkey was tired of trees,
so he followed Little Bear.

Further on, Little Bear saw some crumbling ruins.
A family of jaguars was basking in the sun.

'Where are you going?' they asked.

'To the top of the mountain to explore,' said Little Bear. 'Do you want to come with me?'

'Not just yet,' yawned the jaguars,
'we're much too sleepy.'

So Little Bear went on his way.

But one little jaguar was wide awake,
so he followed Little Bear.

Soon Little Bear met some woolly llamas,
grazing on a grassy slope.

'Where are you going?' asked the llamas.

'To the top of the
mountain,' said Little Bear.
'Do you want to
come with me?'

'Later, later, later,'
grunted the llamas.
'We're too hungry.'

So Little Bear went on his way.

But one little llama had already eaten enough grass
for two little llamas, so he followed Little Bear.

and higher.

and higher

Little Bear climbed higher

The top of the mountain was hidden
by thick, white cloud.
Little Bear felt cold and alone.

Then he heard a noise behind him.

'Surprise!'

There were little ant,
little monkey,
little jaguar and
little llama.

And together
they danced and played …

… and played and danced
until the sun went to bed.